ABC
TOY CHEST

By David Korr
Illustrated by Tom Cooke

A SESAME STREET/READER'S DIGEST KIDS BOOK

Published by Reader's Digest Young Families, Inc.,
in cooperation with Children's Television Workshop

Herry is looking for something
in his toy chest.
What do you suppose it is?

Well, it's not his accordion.

Accordion

It's not his barbell.

Barbell

It's not his camera . . .

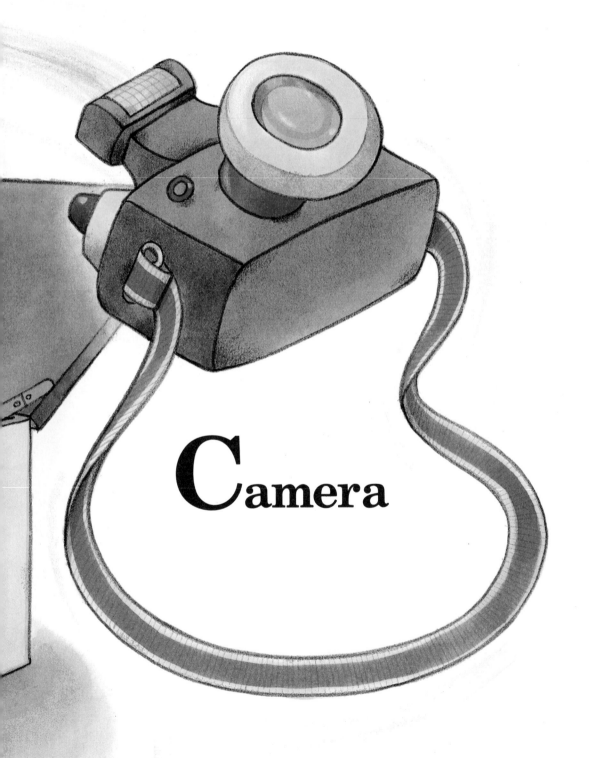

Camera

or his dandy dancing doll.

Doll

It's not his toy elephant, either.

Elephant

Is it his fire truck or his galoshes?

Fire truck

Galoshes

Is it his hat?

Hat

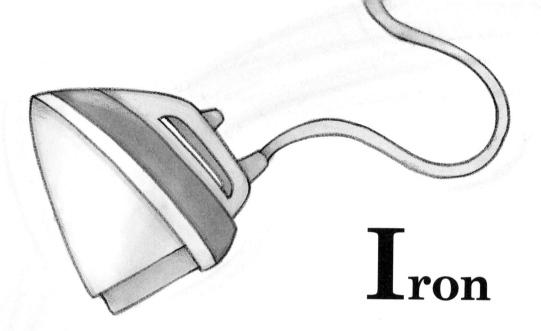

Iron

No, and it's not his iron or the jacket he wears when he goes roller-skating.

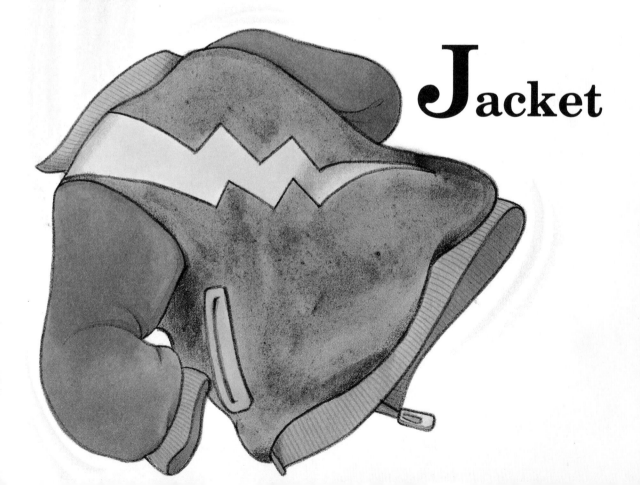

Jacket

Well, it's not his kite.

Kite

Lamp

Is Herry looking for his lamp
or his mailbox with a nest inside?

Mailbox

Nest

Or his old orange owl?

Owl

His paper-bag puppet?

Puppet

What is he looking for?
It's clearly not his quilt.

Quilt

And it's not his radio.

Radio

It's not his toy stove.

Stove

Or his tambourine. And there
goes his long underwear.
It's not that, either.

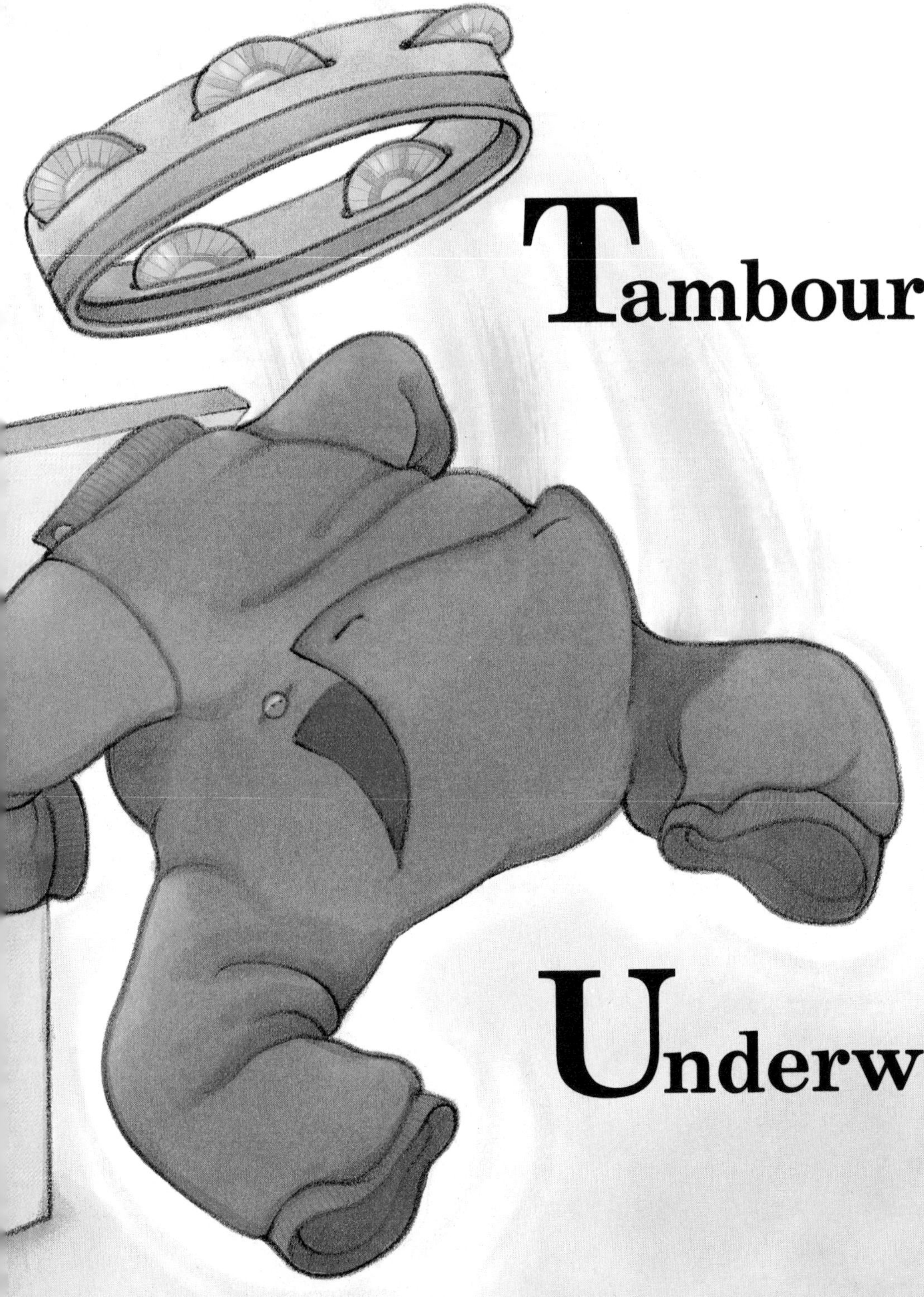

Tambourine

Underwear

Well, now we know it's not his valentine or his watch. Wait. It's probably his xylophone!

Valentine

Watch

Whoops! It's not his xylophone after all, or his yo-yo. What could it be?

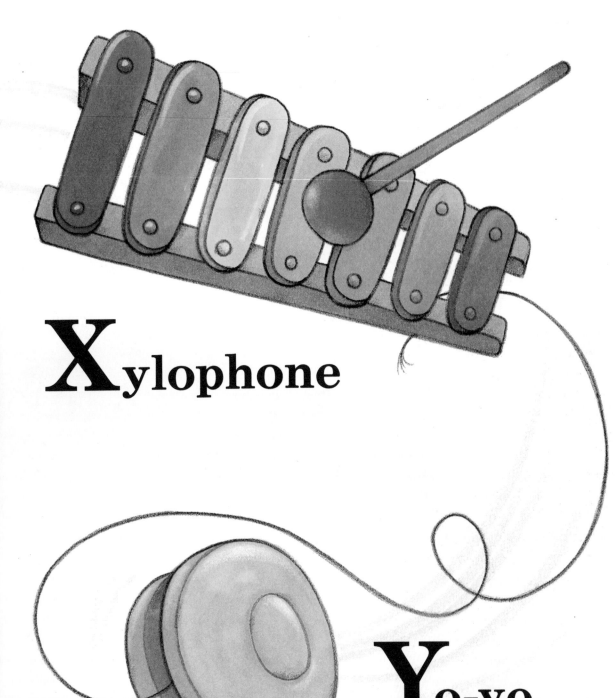

Xylophone

Yo-yo

s not his toy zebra.

Zebra

Look! He's found it!
What is it, Herry? What is it?

Why, it's his Alphabet Book!